Good Dog, Aggie

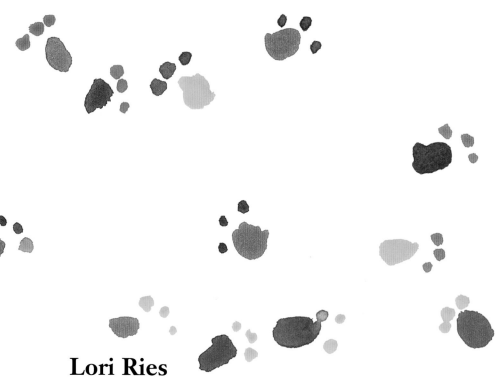

Lori Ries

Illustrated by Frank W. Dormer

ini Charlesbridge

To David, Dan, Katie, Jennifer, and Pupster—L. R.

To the Naked Lads: Chris, Sam, and Max—F. W. D

First paperback edition 2012
Text copyright © 2009 by Lori Ries
Illustrations copyright © 2009 by Frank W. Dormer
All rights reserved, including the right of reproduction in whole or in part in any form.
Charlesbridge and colophon are registered trademarks of Charlesbridge Publishing, Inc.

Published by Charlesbridge
85 Main Street
Watertown, MA 02472
(617) 926-0329
www.charlesbridge.com

Library of Congress Cataloging-in-Publication Data
Ries, Lori.
    Good dog, Aggie / Lori Ries ; illustrated by Frank W. Dormer.
        p. cm.
    Summary: When Aggie the dog does not mind, Ben takes her to obedience school which ends in disaster, but while practicing at home one day Ben realizes what really motivates Aggie to mind.
        ISBN 978-1-57091-645-8 (reinforced for library use)
        ISBN 978-1-57091-646-5 (softcover)
    [1. Dogs—Fiction. 2. Pets—Fiction. 3. Obedience—Fiction.]
    I. Dormer, Frank W., ill. II. Title.
    PZ7.R429Go 2009
    [E]—dc22   2008010651

Printed in Singapore
(hc) 10 9 8 7 6 5 4 3 2 1
(sc) 10 9 8 7 6 5 4 3 2 1

Illustrations done in pen and ink and watercolor on 140-lb. cold-press Winsor and
    Newton paper
Display type set in Tabitha and text type set in Janson
Color separations by Chroma Graphics, Singapore
Printed and bound September 2011 by Imago in Singapore
Production supervision by Brian G. Walker
Designed by Susan Mallory Sherman

Aggie at School

Aggie is a good dog.

She runs fast.

She is a good eater.

But she does not listen.

"Bring that back," I say. "I need that for school!"

"My dog ate my homework," I say.
My teacher does not believe me.

After school I take Aggie outside.
We have a talk.
"You are a good dog, Aggie,
but you do not obey.
You do not come when I say come.
You do not sit when I say sit.
I am going to send you to school.
Doggie school."
"Ruff!" Aggie says.

Doggie school is at the pet shop.

Daddy takes us there.

There are big dogs, little dogs, spotted
dogs, scratching dogs.
Aggie sits on the floor. I sit on a chair.
The teacher is very nice.
She pats all the dogs on the head.
Aggie jumps up.
"No jumping," the teacher says.

The teacher gives us a treat to hold.
"First we will learn SIT," she says.
She shows us how with her dog.
Aggie sniffs my hand. She tries to take
the treat.
"No, no, Aggie," I say.
It is our turn. "Sit," I say.
Aggie does not. She jumps up.
"No, no, Aggie," I say. "It is not time
to play."

The teacher gives us another treat.
"Now we will learn STAY," she says.

She shows us how with her dog.
It is our turn. Aggie sees the treat.
"Sit," I say.
She does.

"Stay," I say.
Aggie does not. She sees another treat.
That treat is closer. Aggie jumps up
and runs to it.

"No, no, Aggie!" I say. "That treat
is not for you!"

Aggie runs.

She runs under one dog.

She jumps over another dog.

Now all the dogs run. They run and bark.
The treats fly up, up, up.

All the dogs stop.

The teacher gives me a box of treats.
"You teach Aggie at home," she says.

"I think Aggie is going to like school," I tell Daddy.

Aggie in Training

I fill my pockets with treats.
"We will work today," I tell Aggie.
"We will work on SIT and STAY."

"Sit, Aggie," I say.
Aggie sits. I give her a treat.
"Stay," I say.
Aggie does not. She sees something.
She sees something gray.

"Ruff! Ruff!" Aggie runs fast.
"Come back!" I say.
The squirrel jumps into the tree.

I take Aggie back to the yard.
"Squirrels are not for you," I say.
I am ready to try again. "Sit," I say.

Aggie does not. She hears something.
She hears something green.
"Do not eat the grasshopper, Aggie."
Aggie sniffs. The grasshopper jumps.
Aggie jumps, too!
"Silly Aggie," I say, "grasshoppers are
not for you."

Training is hard work.
I stop to scratch Aggie's ears.
"Come here, Ben!" Mr. Thomas calls.
"Come let me see Aggie!"

"Yes, sir," I say. "But you cannot see Aggie. You cannot see."

"I see with my hands," Mr. Thomas says. "Aggie is a fine dog! Soft coat, floppy ears . . ."

Mr. Thomas laughs. "And of course, a long, wet tongue!"

Mr. Thomas shows me how to hold the
treat high so Aggie can't take it.
"Sit," I say.
Aggie sits.

"Stay," I say.

Mr. Thomas holds Aggie while I back away.
Then Mr. Thomas backs away, too.
Aggie stays. She sniffs. She smells
something. Aggie smells something orange.
"Ruff! Ruff!" Aggie runs and runs.
"Oh, Aggie, not again!" I say.
"Hisssss!" says the cat. It jumps on top of
the fence.

I take Aggie back to Mr. Thomas.

"Aggie will not learn," I say.

"She will learn," Mr. Thomas says.

"But it will take time."

"Maybe Aggie does not like SIT," I say.

"Maybe she does not like STAY."

My red ball rolls out of my pocket.

Mr. Thomas hands me my red ball.

"Maybe she likes playing fetch,"
he says.

29

"Fetch, Aggie!" I say.
Aggie runs fast.
Aggie is a good dog.
And she will learn.

Someday.

A Bad Dog

"Today we will go to the park," I say.
"We will practice SIT and STAY."
I clip Aggie's leash to her collar.
We pass the bookstore.
We pass the shoe store.
At the hat store, we see a lady.
"What a cute dog!" the lady says.
"Does your dog do tricks?"
"She is learning SIT and STAY," I tell
the lady.
"Sit, Aggie," I say.
Aggie sits.

35

"Stay, Aggie."
She does not. Aggie sees something.
She sees a dog.
"RUFF!" says Aggie.
The leash slips out of my hand.

"RUFF! RUFF! RUFF!" says Aggie.
Now she sees three dogs!
"No, Aggie!" I say.

Aggie runs through the store. I run
after her.
The hats fly up, up, up. One lands on
her head.
"No! No!" I say. "That hat is not
for you!"

Aggie runs back to the dog. "RUFF!"
she says.
Aggie sees three dogs, and three hats!
"Out!" says the lady.

Aggie runs and runs. The hat flies off
her head.

"Aggie!" I yell. "You are a bad dog!"
Aggie stops. She looks sad.
I pick up her leash.
I am sad, too.
I do not want a bad dog.
I do not want Aggie to do bad things.

We walk to the park.
I sit on a bench. Aggie sits next to me.
"I am sorry," I say. "You are not a
bad dog. But you must learn."
Aggie looks at me.
She wags her tail and tugs at my shirt.
The red ball sits in my pocket.
I pull it out.

"This? You want this?" I say.
"Ruff!" says Aggie.
I hold the ball up high.
"Sit, Aggie," I say. Aggie sits.

43

"Stay," I say.

Aggie does. She stays watching the ball.

"Get it, Aggie! Get the ball!" I throw it hard.

Aggie runs and runs. She comes back with the red ball.

"Sit, Aggie," I say.
She does.
"Stay," I say.
Aggie stays. She stays and stays watching
the ball.
"Get the ball, Aggie!" She runs and runs.
Aggie brings me the ball and sits like
a good dog.
She sits and stays and runs after the
red ball.

"Good girl, Aggie!" I tell her.
"You are a good dog!"